Disney Junior
MUPPET BABIES

Hatastrophe

W9-AWA-304

Adapted by Laura Sreebny
Based on the episode written by Laura Sreebny
Illustrated by Character Building Studio

🅖 A GOLDEN BOOK • NEW YORK

ISBN 978-0-7364-3995-4 (trade) ·
Printed in the Unit
10 9 8 7

Jul 2019

The Muppet Babies are playing outside.

"Watch this!" says Fozzie. He tosses his hat into the air and it flies **up, up, up!**

"Wow!" says Kermit.

Kermit asks Fozzie if he can play with the hat.
"Sure!" says Fozzie.

Soon everyone goes inside—except Kermit. He stays in the backyard and tosses Fozzie's hat in the air over and over again, until . . .

. . . the hat flies over the fence and into the neighbors' yard!

"Nooo!" cries Kermit.

He has to get the hat back.

Kermit climbs to the top of the fence and tries using a fishing pole to get the hat. The neighbors see him.

"Are you fishing for a boo-boo?" asks Mr. Statler.
"You could get hurt up there!" says Mr. Waldorf.

Uh-oh. Here comes Fozzie!
Kermit doesn't want him to know about
the hat, so he runs away.

Kermit calls Gonzo, Piggy, Animal, and Summer to the tree house.

"Will you help me get Fozzie's hat back?" he asks them.

"Can I come up, too?" Fozzie calls from the ground.
"Uh . . . not until you guess the password!" calls Kermit.
"Pineapple? Jellyfish? Hot dog?" guesses Fozzie.
"Nope, but you're getting closer," says Kermit as he and
the other Muppet Babies sneak down from the tree house.

"LET THE RESCUE MISSION BEGIN!"

Kermit tells his friends.

The Muppet Babies imagine they are spies as they sneak into Mr. Statler and Mr. Waldorf's yard.

Piggy karate-chops through the fence.

"HIIIIIIIII-YA!"

she says.

Summer and Gonzo push a big statue across the yard. They block the neighbors' view from their house.

"Watch out for the security lasers!" warns Kermit.

The friends **tiptoe, leap,** and **crawl** around the beams.

"The hat! The hat!" cries Animal when he sees it. He gives Kermit a boost.

Kermit reaches **up, up, up!** He almost has the hat, when—

"Hey!" shouts Mr. Statler.

"Stay off that fence!" yells Mr. Waldorf.

Fozzie hears them and comes running over.

"Why is everyone playing without me?" he asks. "I can be fun, too!"

Kermit feels terrible. He has lost Fozzie's hat *and* hurt his feelings.

Kermit finally tells Fozzie the truth.

"I didn't want you to know I lost your hat. I'm sorry, Fozzie," he says.

"That's okay!" says Fozzie. "I can get another hat, but I can't get another best friend."

A few minutes later, Miss Nanny comes to the
playroom with a surprise. It's Fozzie's hat!

"Kermit, I'm glad you told me this was in Mr. Statler
and Mr. Waldorf's yard," says Miss Nanny. "When I rang
their doorbell and told them, they were happy to give
it back."

Now Kermit and Fozzie can
play with the hat together—
indoors!